I0764465

A challenge for Maree

More Books from Macy & JC

TALES OF A TEENAGE ALIEN HUMAN HYBRID

THE ALIEN'S DAUGHTER

THE HYBRID CHALLENGE

COMING SOON

THE HUMAN COMPLICATION

SILVER CITY PRINCESSES

CINDY'S DEMANDING DAY

A CHALLENGE FOR MAREE

COMING SOON

RISA'S SECRET WEAPON

SILVER CITY PRINCESS STORIES

BOOK TWO

MACY MORROWS

JC MORROWS

S&G PUBLISHING

A Challenge For Maree

S&G Publishing, Knoxville, TN
www.sgpublish.com

S&G Publishing, Knoxville, TN
www.sgpublish.com

Scripture quotations are from the Holy Bible (KJV)

Library of Congress Cataloging-in-Publication Data

Morrows, Macy & Morrows, JC

A Challenge For Maree / Macy Morrows, JC Morrows

1. Middle Grade / Fiction / Religious / Christian / Fairy Tales. 2. Middle Grade / Fiction / Fantasy / Fairy Tales. 3. Middle Grade / Fiction / Fantasy. 4. Middle Grade / Fiction / Science Fiction & Fantasy.

ISBN: 978-1948733502

2019932033

First Edition: 2019

PRINTED AND BOUND IN THE UNITED STATES OF AMERICA

For Mom

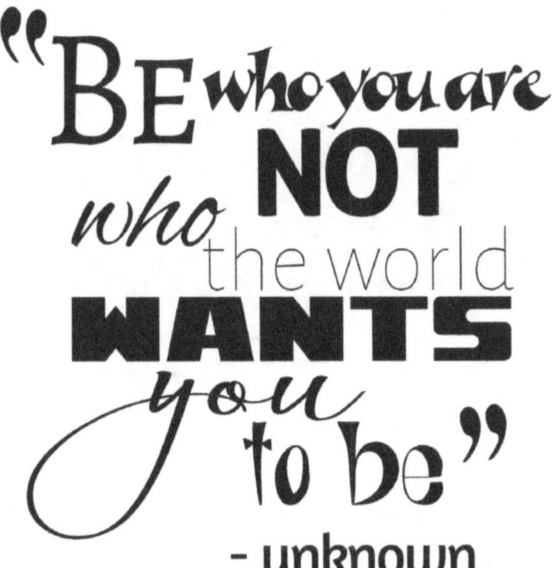
"BE who you are
NOT
who the world
WANTS
you
to be"
- unknown

Chapter One

Maree nocked her arrow, sited the target, took a deep breath, closed her eyes, and let the arrow fly.

"Maree, what are you doing out here? We have to leave soon. You are not even ready."

Maree let out a huff of breath as her opportunity to hear the satisfying thump of an arrow meeting it's target was lost with the sound of her mother's voice.

She turned with a complaint on her lips, but the look of disappointment which always seemed to grace her mother's delicate features when she was near stopped her, and she looked down at the ground as shame colored her cheeks.

If there were just some way she could make her mother happy without turning herself into someone she was not. . .

"Coming, Mum." She collected her

bow and quiver of arrows, never once turning to look at the target behind her.

The satisfaction of a bullseye was soured for her if she didn't get to hear the arrow shaft sinking home.

“Maree, did you really have to sneak off this morning, when we still have so much to do before we leave this afternoon?” Her mother's voice was filled with anger and annoyance.

Maree wanted to stamp her foot and scream, but she held it in. . . as always.

“I am sorry, Mum. I'll be ready before you know it.” With that, she raced off to her room, gritting her teeth at the huff of surprise she heard before she was far enough away from her mother.

She rushed into the house, not bothering to slow down at the started looks she received or even for her mother's voice, following her as she ran up the stairs.

When she reached the second floor, her steps slowed a little, but she still hurried, not wanting to be stopped.

Only once she reached her room, did she stop, and flop onto her bed, dropping bow and quiver carefully beside her on the soft mattress.

She lay there, looking up at the ceiling and wishing she could be what her mother wanted her to be and still somehow be herself.

I don't know why they even want me

to go on this stupid trip. I'll just embarrass them.

She sat up, looking at her reflection in the enormous mirror over her wide dresser. Her bright red hair curled tightly in messy ringlets that went everywhere at once. Her face was darkened from the sun, making each and every freckle stand out in sharp relief.

She had tried the makeup her mother had bought to cover the freckles, but it never looked as good when Maree applied it. And she brushed her hair every single day, just like Mum said she should, but it never mattered. Her curls bounced right back into a crazy mess of corkscrews that refused to be tamed.

Why couldn't I have been born a boy? If I were a boy, no one would care that I'd rather practice archery or climb trees in the wood behind our house.

She envied her younger brothers their freedom. They raced through the house without anyone making a fuss over it. And they constantly tracked in mud and all sorts of dirt. But, because they were boys, no one made a big deal about any of it.

It's just not fair.

Chapter Two

Fortunately, they were not late leaving for the airport.

Maree didn't even have words with her mother over running through the house.

When she came down with her bags,

two that her mother had packed for her and one that she had packed for herself, no one said a word about her taking too long or not being ready on time.

They simply took her bags and loaded them into the car. And then Mum was rushing them all out.

It was only later on the plane, thankfully when they were mostly alone, that her mother spoke to her about her behavior that morning.

"Maree dear, you will remember to be on your absolute best behavior while we are away, won't you?"

While the heat of embarrassment lit up Maree's freckled cheeks, she squirmed in the enormous, overstuffed chair of the fancy jet some country or other had sent for their trip.

It wasn't as if she meant to be on her worst behavior most of the time. She just did the things she enjoyed, and far too often, it ended up either embarrassing her parents—or else her timing was terrible.

Like this morning.

To her mother, though, she kept as close to the truth as possible without making a promise she couldn't keep.

"I will do my absolute best not to embarrass you, Mum."

Maree was surprised when her mother leaned forward to embrace her.

When she moved back a bit later, Maree was even more surprised to see tears in her mother's eyes, though none fell. Her mother never cried.

"Darling girl, you are not an embarrassment to me or to your father. Please never think that. We only ask you to behave the way we do because we love you, and want the best for you."

Maree sat back, but said nothing. Between the unexpected hug, the tears, and her mother's fierce tone of voice, she was more confused than ever.

From the disappointment she was used to seeing on her mother's face when she found Maree doing anything she deemed to be unladylike, it did not feel like it could possibly be true that she was never an embarrassment to her parents.

But she was not about to argue with

her mother, especially with the presence of tears.

Mother never ever cries.

At least, Maree could not remember a time she had ever seen her mother cry. She couldn't even remember a time she had seen her mother with tears in her eyes, but it was no surprise that she had kept them from falling.

Her mother never made mistakes, never acted in an unladylike way, never raised her voice, never said or did the wrong thing; at least not that Maree could remember.

It was one reason her mother's disappointment was never a surprise. Maree expected it.

How could such a perfect mother not

be disappointed or embarrassed by a daughter who could never do anything right?

Chapter Three

Mother had said little else to Maree about her behavior for the rest of the plane ride.

However, when the pilot had announced they would be landing soon, she had ushered Maree into a small room to change her clothes and force a brush through her unruly hair—and when that didn't work, her mother used a half dozen hair clips to tame it somewhat.

When the plane landed, Maree stayed in her seat, though she was itching to be up and looking out the window at this place she had never been before.

She could only think that, perhaps if she sat still, her hair might not have a chance to tangle—and her fancy dress would not get dirty or wrinkled.

Fortunately, it was only a few minutes before the pilot stepped out of the cockpit and announced they could deplane.

Maree struggled with the urge to roll

her eyes at his fancy words.

Don't know why he can't just say we can get off the plane now.

But then, sometimes grown ups were just weird.

They seemed to have a habit of doing things the hard way, saying things in weird ways, either using fancy words or using way more words than they really needed to use.

She didn't understand a bit of it. And she certainly didn't understand why her mother expected her to learn to speak and act the same way.

After all, she had years before she would be an adult. She wanted to enjoy being a young girl for as long as she possibly could.

Not that anyone was going to make that easy for her.

When her parents finally started off the plane, she stood to follow them, putting her younger brothers between them like they always did.

It was always better to have the three mischievous boys in between her mother and her father, where they could easily grab hold if the boys looked about to run off and get into trouble.

Fortunately, none of them ran off in a direction opposite to their parents. And when she stepped out into the open air outside the plane, she was sure she knew why.

The place where they had landed was beautiful. In front of them, there was a large airport. And on both sides, runways stretched out almost as far as one could see.

But beyond that, the view was beautiful, from the mountains in the distance to the green that stretched out in every direction. There was more green than she could ever remember seeing in one place. And the color was different somehow from the grass in their own yard or even from the park near their house.

Feeling more at home than she ever had before, Maree breathed deeply—and even with planes all around, the air was wonderful.

"Come on, Maree. It's time to go." The youngest of her three brothers was pulling at her hand insistently.

She only smiled as she let him pull her down the tall set of metal stairs that had been pushed up against the plane.

He moved quickly, and Maree struggled against his strength and the excitement showing in his movements.

There was no way she would start out her time in this country by falling down a set of metal steps.

Not only would it put her mother's claim to a test immediately. It would also put a stop to any sight-seeing Maree intended to do while they were here.

Her dad's job with the government had sent them to a lot of different countries in her young life, but this was their first visit to the country of her

Dad's ancestors.

She was determined to enjoy every minute of it.

Chapter Four

Thankfully, Maree managed to get down the stairs without an incident. . . and through the airport, as well.

She even made it through the crowd that had gathered to greet them.

In the car that had been waiting at the curb for them just outside of the airport entrance, Maree finally got the chance to look out the window.

Her brothers had immediately pressed their faces up against one of the side windows, arguing about who had a better spot until Mum had made them settle down.

She and Dad sat on the wide back seat with the representative who had met them at the bottom of the stairs when they got off the plane.

He had walked with them all through the airport, talking to her Dad and Mum the whole time about schedules, and arrangements, and business stuff that Maree had only half listened to.

They were still discussing the proposed schedule they were supposed to follow while they were visiting here, only the man was talking very quietly, like everything was some big secret.

She rolled her eyes at his behavior. It wasn't as if they wouldn't find out about the schedule of everything they were doing anyway. . . especially since they would be doing pretty much everything together.

Mum had made a point of telling Maree that very thing when she had told her about the trip. She had stressed how important it was that Maree be on her absolute best behavior for the entire trip.

At the time, Maree had nodded, and

then went back to the book she'd been reading. Now she was worried.

If she somehow embarrassed her parents during one of the events they were doing together, what chance would she have at doing any sight-seeing by herself?

Probably none.

With that thought in mind, she turned back towards the window, determined to take in as many of the sights as possible, just in case it was the only chance she had.

Maree forgot all about being nervous though, when the car pulled up to their hotel.

She had seen the building as they'd driven through town, and as they had gotten closer, the excitement at seeing a real castle up close had overtaken her.

And then the car had stopped, and a man rushed over to open the car door for them a few moments later.

"We're staying here?"

She did not miss the excitement in Mum's voice when she answered. "Yes, dear, we are. Hurry now."

Mum ushered them all out of the car. When they stepped out, there was already someone taking their bags out of the trunk.

Chapter Five

Everything likely would have been fine if Maree had stayed at the hotel their first full day in Edinburgh.

However, that very morning they were scheduled for a group activity, so of course, they went as a group—and the trouble began.

They had breakfast at the hotel, after which the fancy car picked them up, and brought them to their first family event of the trip.

Mum had picked out a very nice outfit for Maree. Though she was not one bit fond of dresses, she was doing everything possible to hide her feelings about them for this trip, knowing how important it was to Mum and Dad that everything go smoothly.

However, smooth was not in any way a description that could be used for this family outing.

Not more than an hour passed before the first incident brought everyone's attention to Maree, and in the worst possible way.

It had all started off innocently enough. She'd been standing off to the side of the enormous room where her parents had been grandly welcomed, doing her best to draw no attention to herself, when a young man had walked past her.

Determined to go the length of the party unnoticed, she paid him no attention to begin with.

However, when he started to complain about certain people—and it was quite obvious which people he meant—who had turned their backs on their country and gone off to live with. . . she'd no idea what *clatty cuddies* were, but they sounded pretty bad to her. . .

she could no longer ignore him.

No one insulted her Dad.

Still, she did not want to draw the wrong sort of attention, so she was cautious about how she approached him.

To begin with, she only moved a little closer to him and the two boys who stood with him. Then she continued to listen in on their conversation.

They spent a long time talking badly about more than just her Dad. It seemed as if they had some scathing remark for just about every single person attending. . . even her little brothers.

Fists clenched at her sides, it was all Maree could do not to plant one of them in the bully's face.

The nerve he had. . . to be so nasty

about kids—and young kids at that. He certainly deserved a punch in the nose.

But every time she started forward, she was reminded of how solemnly her Mum had reminded her about the importance of this trip.

Not only was Dad here to visit the country of his birth. He was here to kindle a better relationship with that country and the one he called home now.

He had a very important job and she certainly did not want to be responsible for his efforts being anything less than successful.

Not to mention, she did not wish to be an embarrassment to either him or Mum.

So she held her tongue, and kept her fists balled at her sides, though at times it took every ounce of self control she could muster.

Perhaps that was why she missed the signs of trouble. She told herself later that she at least had the reassurance that she did not start the trouble.

She was not the one who had spilled a glass of dark red liquid on the Prime Minister as he walked by, though the young boy who somehow managed to disappear rather quickly afterwards was the only one who could truly attest to that fact.

There was no way to know if it was to her benefit or not, that she was also soaked in the spilling of the drink.

One moment, she was standing there with both hands clenched into tight fists, thinking how delightful it would be to plant a punch right on the end of what most certainly must be a very pointy nose.

Bad guys almost always had pointy noses... or no nose at all.

The next second, she was jumping back from the flood of deep, dark, red liquid splashing up over her fancy green dress and the Prime Minister's light grey suit.

And the very next thing was the expression of horror on her mother's face. Even from across the room, she could see clearly how her Mum's features went from shock at how quickly everything had gone wrong to a mix of un-surprise and the all-too-familiar disappointment.

Chapter Six

Over the next week, Maree barely left the hotel.

Instead, she spent a great deal of time wandering the halls and curling up in chairs mostly tucked away out of sight with the books she had brought with her.

It was not how she had meant to spend her time in the wonderful, beautiful, exciting country her Dad's family had come to America from so many years ago. However, it proved to be the safest course of action.

If she avoided her Mum, and the parties and events she and Dad were already committed to attending, there was no chance of another incident being blamed on her.

However, one afternoon she was quite surprised to look up into the face of none other than the young man who had framed her for his own crime, and left her to deal with the consequences. . . effectively ruining her trip.

"Oy, whacha readin' there?"

Shock was the only explanation Maree could come with to justify why she did not plant her fist in his big, nose pointy nose at that moment.

She could never have expected him to show up in their hotel just then, and talk to her as if they were the best of friends catching up.

"Good book, is it?" He went on as he dropped into the chair beside hers.

She could only nod. Her mind was busy trying to figure out how to handle the situation in front of her.

She could punch him. That was for certain. And he would certainly deserve it. Not only had he gotten her into trouble, he had soaked her dress and the

Prime Minister's suit, effectively putting a damper on the remainder of the evening for both of them, and her family as well.

However, she also knew that if she punched him, no matter how satisfying it might be, her Mum would be disappointed in her—again.

So she went with vague disinterest in the hopes that she could simply discourage him from talking to her, waving the book in front of his nose, but saying nothing.

Hopefully he can take a hint.

After all, if he went away, she would have less reason to punch him, which meant less chance of putting that look back on Mum's face.

He did not take the hint though. In fact, he didn't seem to even recognize her.

"Say, didn't I see ye at the party t'other night?"

She nodded, said nothing, then buried her nose in her book again. He just sat there beside her, watching her as she read.

At least ten minutes passed that way. And she only knew the time because she'd been watching the conveniently placed clock on the wall across the room from them.

He said nothing, so she said nothing. He watched her as she read. Hopefully, he had no idea she was reading the same paragraph over and over again.

When it had been ten minutes, she decided she'd had enough. Either he was going to go away or she was going to punch him.

She put down her book, careful not to take out her irritation with him on the story she had been enjoying until he'd interrupted her.

“Just what do you want?” Maree aimed what she hoped was her most annoyed expression at him.

He looked completely unconcerned, lounging in the chair next to hers, a look on his face that could only be described as haughty, and completely unwilling or unable to take even a simple hint.

Maybe I can hit him just once. Who would know? Nobody, that's who.

There was no one else around, no one else sitting in the comfortable chairs that made up this delightful little sitting area, no one walking past. . . and there hadn't been for some time.

No one would see. No one would know. And he was not exactly the type who would run off and tattle to his Mum.

No, he would be the type to take it like a man. I'm sure of it.

She had actually balled up her fist in preparation, when an image of the expression she so disliked on her mother's sweet face reminded her of how hard she was working not to embarrass her family on the remainder of the trip.

And knowing my luck, someone would walk by just as my fist connected with his ugly face, and it would likely be someone who knows Dad.

She muttered a word she would never utter in her mother's—or her brothers'—presence, and then she purposely unballed her fist. If there was no fist, there might. . . might, mind you, be less temptation.

And he. . . well, he just sat there with that same crooked, smug grin on his face—as if he knew he had just dodged a bullet. . . just as if he knew precisely what she had been planning, and that she'd decided against it, and now he was off the hook, scot free.

She stared at him for another minute

and when he still said nothing—just sat there grinning at her—she picked up her book again. And, with a huff in his general direction, she sat back down and started to read again.

Chapter Seven

Maree never did get anything out of him, though she was shortly spared his presence, at the very least.

Several minutes after she went back to her book, a very loud, more than slightly annoying song began to play somewhere in the general vicinity of his pocket.

He pulled a very expensive-looking smart phone from his pocket—after the song had nearly finished—and tapped a few keys. Then he heaved himself out of the chair and, without a word, he walked away.

She watched his back as his long legs ate up the distance of the long hall. She didn't really mean to. . . and didn't really want to know what it must mean.

But it was a long time until she went back to her book. Not that it mattered much.

Only about five minutes after her mysterious companion left, her brothers appeared, skidding to a halt in three short, oddly-timed halts.

I will never figure out how they do that.

She shook her head as they took a second to catch their breath.

It must be a triplet thing.

By then, almost as one, they launched into speech, not at their top voices, but pretty close.

“Mum said you'd take us swimming today. And we wanna go now.” The words came out in a tumble, just like almost everything they said.

Fortunately, after nearly five years of translating the strange almost-echo way they tended to speak, she understood enough to know what they wanted from her.

Then, in part because she was a big sister and it was part of her job to torture them, and in part because she was genuinely trying to figure out the best thing to do, she sat there for a minute with a pensive expression on her face.

They gave her almost the full minute before they started tugging at different parts of her. Two of them took a hand each and the other pulled at her t-shirt.

"Come on sis, please?"

She laughed. "Okay. Let's go up and put on our suits, then."

That was all they needed. They were whooping as they ran off in the direction of the elevators.

The pool was completely deserted when they arrived, not one person was in the pool, nor one person occupying any of the chairs around it.

She was thankful no one was near the pool a moment later, when all three brothers launched themselves into the pool as hard as possible, each trying to outdo the others, both in the size of their splash and their acrobatics on the way.

Maree rolled her eyes at their antics, but smiled. They knew how to enjoy themselves.

They certainly don't have to worry day and night about disappointing Mum and Dad, like I do.

And why would they? Nothing they had ever done seemed to embarrass Mum or Dad in the least.

Deep down Maree knew that it was entirely possible that at least some of it was because they were only seven. They still had years before Mum would expect them to start acting *grown up.*

But that did not stop her from envying them the ease with which they went through life, blissfully unaware of any of the disappointment that she felt mostly from Mum, but on occasion from Dad, as well.

Shaking her head, Maree reminded herself that they had come down to the pool to swim, to have fun, and to relax. She should not be sitting here wallowing in self-pity.

So she didn't.

She stopped thinking about such things as disappointment and behaviors of any kind and concentrated on having fun.

She watched her brothers as they jumped into the pool again and again, swimming quickly to the side each time after hitting the water and hoisting themselves back out, only to race to the water again.

It went on like that for some time. . . until she was certain they must be wearing themselves out.

And just as she opened her mouth to suggest they go in search of some lunch, the door opened and in walked a group of boys led by one very familiar boy with a snarky smirk she recognized right away.

She snapped her mouth shut immediately. If she suggested they leave now, it would only look like she was running from him and she was not about to give him the satisfaction.

Chapter Eight

Neither he nor the boys with him paid her any attention.

They dropped towels and bags on chairs on the opposite side of the pool from her and then jumped in, behaving much like her young brothers had not an hour ago.

She should be relieved they were ignoring her. She should count her blessings, but something about the entire situation did not sit right.

He had walked up to her earlier, asked her about the book she was reading. He had sought her out.

And then ignored my questions.

That bothered her more than she cared to admit. Why had he sat down beside her, and then ignored her?

There was no good reason she could think of—which meant he must be up to no good.

And given his behavior the other evening, it was no real surprise. Clearly, he was lacking any real manners and got his kicks by making messes and being rude.

When he looked right at her, with that annoying, cocky, self-satisfied smirk of his, she realized she was staring.

Why am I staring at him?

It took no time at all to realize she really had no reason.

Other than being annoyed with him, of course.

He had annoyed her. He had confounded her. And he had gotten her in trouble for something she'd had nothing whatsoever to do with. For that alone, she was determined to figure him out—and return the favor if possible while she was at it.

The thought of watching him, just as embarrassed as she had been during the party, dress covered in some unknown dark liquid, looking for all the world like the culprit who had drenched the Prime Minister, was so wonderful. . . so perfectly delicious, that she laughed.

No sooner had the sound left her than she realized how silly she must look, sitting here and staring off into space, laughing at absolutely nothing.

Not that I care a bit what they think of me.

She told herself she didn't care, but something about her insistence did not ring entirely true.

She did care.

Why did she care?

She shouldn't care. She knew that. She didn't want to care. She did want, desperately, to pay him back in kind, for his rudeness and for getting her into so much trouble, even if that had not been his objective.

“You're not swimming?” His deep voice sounded from very close, throwing her off entirely.

When had he gotten so close? Why was he asking her about swimming?

Because you're at a pool, dummy.

The answer made sense. She knew it did, but there was something about the way he had asked that told her there was more to his question.

She answered as simply as possible. “I'm watching my little brothers.”

She should have known her answer would not be enough for him. Not even a second passed before he shot back, "You can't watch them while you're in the water, too?"

She wanted to snap, to yell, to snarl. Instead, she answered calmly, again using a simple truth.

"It's safer if I don't. I could lose sight of them too easily from the water." It was the truth, just not all of it. She was okay with that.

He was not. "Oh come on, now. They're not going to drown in this pool. It can't be more than four feet at its deepest."

He gestured behind him at the pool, at my brothers splashing around in the pool with his friends, and she could see that she was running out of excuses.

"Why did you wear your swimsuit if you didn't plan to swim?"

His question threw a curve she hadn't expected. She opened her mouth to answer. Nothing came to her. There was no ready answer.

She expected him to push again. Instead, he shrugged and ran to jump in the pool again, surfacing a few seconds later with that same infuriating grin on his face.

She took advantage of the fact that he was not expecting her to jump in, and did exactly that.

When she landed in the water, only inches from him, the grin was completely erased by a look of pure surprise as water swamped him.

She came up laughing.

Chapter Nine

Early the next morning, she sat down at the breakfast table across from her mum and wondered at the cold expression that met her.

I just woke up, for crying out loud. What could I possibly have done already?

Two seconds later, she got her answer. On the front page of the paper her Dad was reading, there was a picture. . . a close up of her and the boy whose name she had finally learned yesterday afternoon at the pool—Dylan.

They were both in the water, and he was very close to her. The angle of the photo almost made it look like their bodies were actually touching, as if she were leaning up against him. She was laughing.

It looked to her like the moment after she had jumped in, hitting him with a huge wave of water, and then came up laughing.

They had not been touching. She

hadn't leaned up against him. She'd been close, sure, but not that close.

The picture must have been snapped using a very long lens, by someone outside of the pool area, who had been watching them.

The headline in all capitals read, *TEEN DIPLOMATIC RELATIONS!* And the way the words were printed, using a slanted, bold print, somehow gave them a look of being sarcastic or mocking.

Heat crept up Maree's neck, and across her cheeks, filling her whole face with physical evidence of her embarrassment and anger.

The words should have meant something good. The phrase diplomatic relations should have shown that the

United States was determined to strengthen their relationship with Scotland, even so much that the families of the diplomats were working at it.

But with that picture, it looked more like teens partying, being naughty. . . doing bad things. There was absolutely nothing positive about this.

It was another thing that she had done, without meaning to, that would embarrass her family and make Dad's job here more difficult.

“Would it help to say that is not at all what it looks like?” Her voice came out much quieter than she intended, but she made no effort to speak louder, recognizing that it might work to her advantage.

Did she sound as embarrassed as she felt? Would Mum take it that way?

Would Dad?

No one answered for several long, tense minutes. Her mother sipped coffee. Her dad read his paper.

To be completely fair, she knew—as low as she'd spoken—he honestly might not have even heard her.

But her mother had. She proved it a moment later—and when she did speak, her voice was dangerously quiet, smooth in a way that always meant trouble.

"I would suggest you stay here today, but we have a very important event that we cannot miss."

"I don't have to. . ." Maree started to offer to miss it anyway, but her mother cut her off.

"No, you have to be there too. Everyone is bringing their family. It is an important day." She pushed back from the table then, mumbled something about seeing to their clothes, and then she was gone.

Maree nearly turned to watch her go, but knew it would not improve her mood one bit to see the ramrod straight posture that always meant her mother was thinking about how un-ladylike her only daughter was.

"Don't mind your mother, sweet pea. You know how she worries about appearances." A moment later he added. "It's the Brit in her. They're so proper, you know."

"I know." Maree answered with a quiet huff.

Her mother was proper before she was anything else. . . before she was affectionate, before she was proud of them or their accomplishments, before she showed any emotion whatsoever.

And her determination to always be proper left emotions out of most parental interactions. . . or at least, the ones involving Maree.

"I suppose I'd better go and get ready." Her appetite gone, Maree pushed away from the table as well, following her mother towards the large bedroom that was somehow all hers.

When she passed her Dad, he laid his paper down and pulled her into his arms for a tight hug. She snuggled close, letting out a long, shaky breath as she burrowed into the warmth of his embrace; the one place in the world where she always felt safe.

It was several minutes before he spoke. “She does what she does because she believes it's the right thing. She only wants the best for you.” When Maree only nodded, he went on. “We both do.”

She looked up with only a slightly shaky smile then. “I know, Da. Thanks!” She threw her arms around him then and squeezed.

Chapter Ten

Several hours later, Maree was actually glad Mum had made her come with them.

The event she had been so worried about turned out to be pure enjoyment for Maree and her young brothers.

The first hour had been a mock tournament, with men done up as knights, wearing armor that truly looked like the real thing.

They paraded in on their horses, went through the motions of several complex ceremonies, each equally fascinating.

And then came the archery.

When the last ceremony had been completed, when the last of the parades had ended, a man with a high pitched voice stepped up onto the platform off to one side of the field.

He announced into a microphone that refreshments would be served under a tent at one side of the field while the next portion was set up.

Being special guests of the country,

Maree's family certainly could have moved to the head of the line. However, being a diplomat family who never took such advantage, they moved with the group of people they'd been seated with, taking their place in line with everyone else.

Maree barely took her eyes off the field, her attention commanded by what was being carried out into the open area and placed at regular intervals.

She knew precisely what they would be watching when they returned, and was already certain this day would be the highlight of their trip for her.

It was all she could do, when they moved down the steps at the end of the tiers of seats and she could no longer see the field, to continue to follow her family.

As they moved towards the large white tent, she stood on her tip toes and craned her neck, trying to catch a glimpse again.

"Don't get your hopes up. None of them are very good." The voice beside her was annoyingly familiar, and she closed her mouth over the response that leaped to her tongue, her teeth shutting with a hard click.

How long until her parents saw who was standing beside her, keeping pace with her, talking to her?

Would her mother be more angry if she were to talk to him. . . or if she continued to ignore his very presence?

There was no way to know whether her mother would prefer rudeness to scandal and the indecision made Maree want to scream, more just now than any other time.

This was the boy who had gotten her into major trouble twice now—and likely would again. . . soon.

What do I do?

"I tried to tell them I should be on the field today. Dad just wouldn't listen."

She looked over to see him shaking his head, that same maddening crooked grin of his occupying his otherwise solemn face.

"Oh, well." And then he shrugged, as if none of it mattered one bit.

Someone behind them in line made a

sound in their throat and Maree realized she was standing still, holding up the line.

She turned to see where the line had moved, and stepped forward, moving closer to her father. She had a moment to be thankful her mum and brothers were in front of Dad.

At least they wouldn't see immediately whose company she was keeping.

She also won't see immediately that I'm being rude.

The thought was oddly freeing. She couldn't make him go away, but she didn't have to talk to him. . . at least, not until her mum saw that she wasn't.

With that in mind, she turned away

from him and stepped forward again, following on the heels of her dad.

"It's just as well, I suppose. It would be wasted on this crowd. Most of the people here wouldn't know a good show if they saw one."

Maree cringed at his words. How did he seem to know precisely what to say to get a reaction out of her?

First he insults his own people. Then he brags outrageously. Now he's insulting my people.

There was no doubt he was insulting them, if nothing else as part of the crowd who weren't his people, since he very well knew they came from America. Though he didn't seem to know of their heritage.

Should she let him in on it. . . or wait until her father saw him there and spoke with the heavy brogue that would bely his ancestry?

The decision was made for her a second later when her dad did just that. He turned to speak to Maree and must have seen who was behind her.

“Well, then. Just the young man I've been wanting to meet.” He turned and offered a hand to the young man behind her.

Maree could only shake her head in surprise. Was this the same man who had looked so uncomfortable over his morning paper at the breakfast table?

It couldn't be. . . could it?

Nevertheless, he put out his hand—

and Dylan took it.

"How do you do, sir?"

That was it. No surprise. No shock. No hesitation. He shook her father's hand and greeted him as an equal, not as a grown up or a parent, just as another man.

Maree simply stood there, watching the two exchange pleasantries, listened as her dad chatted, and watched as he smiled and laughed with him.

She had no idea what to make of it. . . any of it. It was as if the picture in the newspaper didn't exist, as if he were a good friend of hers that they'd been waiting to meet, someone important.

He'd gotten her into trouble and her dad was being nice to him.

She shook her head and moved around Dad to pick up a plate. Let them chat. She wasn't getting in the middle of it.

They chatted all through the line like old friends who hadn't seen each other in years.

She filled her plate and then moved away to find a place to sit, hoping against hope that she could get through the break without any more trouble.

She did not want to miss the archery demonstration, no matter Dylan's opinion of the skill level of those involved.

Chapter Eleven

After refreshments, the same man who had announced the break appeared again.

This time she got a much better look at him while he made his announcement. He was dressed like a page of the old court, though he did not resemble any page she'd every seen, except one in a delightfully silly cartoon she remembered her mother letting them watch years ago.He spoke loudly, without aid of a microphone this time, announcing that the tournament would continue in twenty minutes. Then he was gone, blending into the crowd that was suddenly formed in the space he had just vacated.

She watched as the people surged after him.

No doubt they want to be certain they get their seats back.

The thought was a sour one again, ruined by what Dylan had said earlier.

How dare he suggest that the show was just that—a show, and a subpar one at that.

Clearly he was a young man who acted without thought as to how his actions could or would affect others around him.

Just one more reason to detest him.

She frowned as she followed the crowd, who simply reversed the course they had taken over a half an hour ago.

It felt completely ridiculous and unfair to her that Dylan had gotten her into trouble twice now, and yet her own father greeted him like he was a family friend, someone important.

When she reached the box area where they had been seated earlier, she sat in one of the seats her brothers had been in before.

The seat was at the front of the box, with a much better view of the field—and she wanted to see the archery demonstration.

It felt like a very long time until her family moved into the box and took their seats. Thankfully, none of the boys argued with her about the change in seating. They just took the seats left over and leaned forward in clear expectation.

Not that she blamed them. She was just as excited as they were to watch. And finally, a line of archers made their way onto the field. They took positions and then, one by one, they shot.

Not one of them hit the center of

their target. She let out a huff of breath in irritation.

He was right.

It did not help that the crowd around them erupted into thunderous applause.

Clearly none of them were actually archers. . . or indeed observant of the actual skill of those on the field.

What was worse, at that moment, she happened to look right at Dylan, who wore an expression that basically said, *"I told you so."*

Maree deliberately looked away, back to the more than slightly disappointing demonstration on the field in front of them.

They might not be particularly skilled, but there was still something to be enjoyed in watching her favorite past-time. Just the graceful arc of an arrow leaving the bow was worth watching.

And I can always look away before the arrow reaches its target.

When the demonstration was over, and most of the spectators had left the stands, Maree wandered over to the targets that were still set up on the field.

A few of the shots had been close, but not one arrow had struck dead center.

How she wished there had been some

way for her to be in the line of archers. She would have hit dead center. At the very least, every shot would have been in the center circle.

Why did they not have at least one skilled archer on the field?

Certainly there must be skilled archers available for such a demonstration.

Why, even Dylan had made the comment that he had offered to be one of them. She was fairly certain he had been bragging about his considerable skill, but it was difficult to imagine that he would not have been at least a little better than those who had been chosen.

Chapter Twelve

Before her family left the field, Maree was again surprised by Dylan's unexpected appearance.

He walked out onto the field, holding two long bows and a quiver of arrows.

He stopped at the firing line and motioned to her when she made no move towards him.

Looking to her parents, she could see they were caught up in their conversation and the boys were chasing each other along the lowest rows of seats where they had sat just a few minutes ago.

Surely there would be no harm in participating. . . There were very few people around, and none of them were paying any attention to her or the remaining targets on the field.

Making up her mind, she stepped closer and pulled arrows from two of the targets.

When they were both clear, she made

her way to the other end of the field where Dylan stood, that stupid grin on his crooked face.

How had he judged her so accurately, somehow knowing that she would be unable to leave the field once he had essentially challenged her?

She looked away from him, focusing her attention on the bunch of arrows in her hands. They all looked to be in good enough shape to use again. Every head held its shape. Every shaft was intact.

She nodded her head somewhat absently at her own assessment of what would shortly become her own ammunition.

When she reached the spot where Dylan stood, she did not smile. . . or speak. She dropped the arrows into a small bin that one of the archers had been using earlier in place of a quiver and then nodded to Dylan when he handed her one of the bows.

A moment later, he handed her a leather bracer and glove. She took her time putting them on, watching him as he put his own on as well.

Once everything was in place, he turned towards her and spoke. “Ladies first.” And since it was not a tournament, she accepted his offer.

Turning towards the target, she stepped into her stance and began to line up the shot, testing the bow as she nocked her arrow and pulled back experimentally on the bow string.

When she let the first arrow fly, she honestly did not expect it to hit dead center. Using an unfamiliar bow and arrows, no one would have faulted her for an off-center shot.

However, the arrow buried itself deep into the very center of her target and she flushed with pleasure. She turned to Dylan with a smile on her face, only to meet her mother's usual disappointed expression.

Dylan did not see it, and took his turn shooting.

As hers had, his arrow hit dead center of his target on the first shot, and she was forced to admit, whether he had been bragging or not earlier, he was a skilled archer.

His whoop of delight distracted her mother and got the attention of her father, who started walking toward them—and her brothers, who came skidding to a halt just beside them a few moments later.

Whoever it was her parents were speaking with must also have decided it was worth a look as well, because they followed the small entourage as they made their way back across the field.

"That was very well done, lad." Her father turned to her then. "I do believe you might have found someone who just might be a match for you, Maree." He smiled at her as he said it.

She didn't answer, but she did smile at her father. . . not Dylan. It had not escaped her notice that her father had said match. So, he didn't think Dylan could be more skilled. He simply thought Dylan might have the same amount of skill. . . and he had said might, not definitely.

"Best of five?" She said, not waiting for the answer before turning back to the target.

When no one told her not to, she took her stance again, nocked an arrow, sited the target and then breathed in as she closed her eyes.

She only opened her eyes again after letting the arrow fly, a grin already spreading across her face as the arrow struck the target so close to the first, that it shoved the shaft sideways.

The stunned silence from all around her was all she needed to know they were all impressed with her shot.

Hmm. Beat that, Dylan.

She didn't say it aloud. She didn't need to. It felt good to know, looking at the expression on his face. . . at the absence *finally* of that stupid grin of his, that there was no chance he actually could outdo the shot.

This is NOT the end. . .

It's just the beginning!

"I will praise thee; for I am fearfully and wonderfully made: marvellous are thy works; and that my soul knoweth right well."

~ Psalms 139:14-16

A NOTE FROM MACY

Magic, wondrous characters, and fantastical stories are only a few of the things I love about Fairy Tales.

And, as much as I love the originals, I love making new stories for the beloved characters we've all grown up with.

I hope readers who enjoy Fairy Tales as much as I do, will enjoy the modern twists my mother and I have added to these much-loved stories.

~ Macy

"For God so loved the world, that He gave His only begotten Son, that whosoever believeth in Him should not perish, but have everlasting life."

~ John 3:16

A NOTE FROM JC

Like most little girls with fanciful imaginations, I have always had a special place in my heart for Fairy tales.

Who doesn't love a world where villains get what's coming to them, good always wins, and little girls are rewarded the truest desires of their hearts in the end?

We don't live in a world where many people get the desires of their hearts, nor a world where good and evil always come out where they should.

That is one reason I write fantasy that follows this all-important formula. We all need that safe place.

~ JC

"Call unto me, and I will answer thee, and shew thee great and mighty things, which thou knowest not."

~ Jeremiah 33:3

ABOUT THE AUTHORS

Macy Morrows is a young girl following in her mother's footsteps, with storytelling, having her head in the clouds, and spending her time in fictional worlds. She fits in better than her mother ever did though. . . and that's not a bad thing

JC Morrows is an author of fantastical fiction filled with faith. She writes about assassins, aliens, dragons, angels, fairy tales, and teenagers trying desperately to survive in post-apocalptic worlds.

She also drinks coffee. . . lots and lots of coffee.

ABOUT THE PUBLISHER

Christian Publishing for HIS GLORY

S&G Publishing offers books with messages that honor Jesus Christ to the world! S&G works with Christian authors to bring you the best in "inspirational" fiction and non-fiction.

S&G is proud to publish a variety of Christian fiction genres:
inspirational romance
young reader
young adult
speculative
historical
suspense

Check out our website at:
sgpublish.com

DON'T MISS BOOK ONE

WELCOME TO SILVER CITY: WHERE HAPPILY EVER AFTER IS STILL A MODERN GIRL'S DREAM!

Meet Cindy, a soft-spoken maid-in-training who secretly wishes she could do a little more than clean the prince's toilets...

As good as orphaned, Cindy works for her step-mother, who owns a high class maid service that caters to the well-to-do families of Silver City.

BOOK ONE OF THE SILVER CITY PRINCESS STORIES

MORE FROM JC & MACY

As if being a teenager isn't hard enough. . .

Can you imagine how it feels to wake up one day and find out that you are not who you thought you were?

If you're anything like me, you know it's hard enough trying to fit in—in high school—without having to deal with the knowledge that your dad is an alien part of the time. I don't even get how you can be an alien part of the time...

As if I don't have enough to deal with. . .

It's crazy enough to find out, the hard way, that you are not who you thought you were.

But to have that kind of bombshell dropped on you, and then — to have your Dad ditch you — leaving you to figure stuff out all by yourself, with a Mom you can't tell anything about what's going on. . .

MORE FROM S&G Publishing

SOPHIE IS A KITTEN WHO FOUND TWO CHILDREN . . . AND DECIDED TO ADOPT THEM AS HER OWN

Read along with Sammy and Macy as they tell the story of finding a little lost kitten, naming her, loving her, and making her part of their (or rather, becoming her own) family.

Enjoy Thanksgiving with them. Read about how Sophie celebrates this fun holiday filled with food, family and mischief.

Then read about how Sophie's family made the move from the big city... and Sophie followed.

Now she has her own house, a big yard, and new kitty friends right next door!

Katie Chupp spends her days at The Sweet Shop, taking care of customers and baking delicious treats... not exactly a profession where one expects to be thrown into the midst of mysteries and mayhem.

But when the bakery is broken into, someone has to find the thief . . . besides finding another place to do the baking and get the orders to the customers.

Is this a random theft, or is the thief trying to ruin the town's Independence Day celebration?

It's the most wonderful time of the year and Katie Chupp is spending her days catering to the holiday rush. With everyone in town ordering special desserts and treats, will Katie be able to find time to finish making gifts for her family and friends?

With a winter chill settling in and Christmas right around the corner, no one would expect a mystery, but a mystery does indeed appear... And this is one mystery that may never be solved...

Amelia Simpkins may be a great cook, and have a head for business, but sweet treats are out of her league and the owner of the Irish Blessings Cafe says it's because she adds the tart to the Sweet Shop's new dessert that Katie Chupp insists is only filled with lemony goodness.

The two shop owners' constant bickering sends sparks flying through Abbott Creek's usual calm... and when Andrew's cafe suffers from some rather unusual pest problems, the town starts taking sides.

It's the time of year when the residents of Abbott Creek give thanks for their blessings.

But Katie is having difficulty deciding whether she should be thankful. . . or careful of the new relationships she has developed over the previous year...

Katie Chupp is not the only person in Abbott Creek looking forward to the most romantic holiday of the year...

But Valentine's Day will not be all hearts and flowers. There are secrets to be kept, feelings to be explored, and difficult decisions to be made — and each one has something to do with the heart.

Will those secrets come between friends? Will the happy couples in Abbott Creek get to celebrate. . . together?

Between babies and budding romances, busy schedules and unexpected gossip, the small town and its residents may never be the same.

Everyone at the Sweet Shop Bakery and the Irish Blessings cafe is worrying over Bella and her baby – and busily trying to convince her to take it easy.

Katie is not the only person in town with some big decisions ahead of her. And the busy summer season is kicked off with a big surprise for everyone.

www.ingramcontent.com/pod-product-compliance
Lightning Source LLC
Chambersburg PA
CBHW070446170726
48291CB00005B/1617

* 9 7 8 1 9 4 8 7 3 3 5 0 2 *